This book
belongs to:
K KNOX

Weekly Reader Children's Book Club Presents

Baby Kermit's Christmas

by
Louise Gikow

• • •

illustrated by
Lauren Attinello

Muppet Press

To my mother and father,
for all their love
–Lauren

This book is a presentation of Weekly Reader Books.
Weekly Reader Books offers book clubs for children
from preschool through high school. For further information
write to: **Weekly Reader Books,**
4343 Equity Drive, Columbus, Ohio 43228.

Published by arrangement with
Muppet Press.

This 1988 Muppet Press book is published by Longmeadow Press.
Printed in U.S.A.

h g f e d c b a

Baby Kermit sat in front of the nursery window, watching the snow fall.

Fine, fat flakes filled the sky, whirling and dancing as they came. The ground was already covered with a thick blanket, but the snow showed no sign of stopping.

It was the night before Christmas, and all the Muppet Babies had left cookies and milk for Santa. Now they dreamed of holly and candy canes and toys in their stockings. Only Kermit was awake. He stared out the window, blinking sleepily.

The snow rose, covering fire hydrants and hedges. It crept quietly up the sides of trees. Soon it would cover the lampposts. Then, perhaps, it would hide even the house from view.

Kermit was worried. What if the snow were so deep that Santa Claus couldn't find the nursery? What would become of Christmas Day? Piggy and Fozzie and Gonzo and Rowlf and Scooter and Skeeter and Animal would be so disappointed.

So Kermit put on his warmest jacket, his red-and-white-striped scarf, his red-and-white-striped mittens, and his red boots. He took his little shovel, too, just in case he had to dig up some snow. Then he quietly opened the window and stepped outside.

The snow had drifted high under the sill, and the world was a mass of white humps and bumps. Kermit looked around. Now he was certain that Santa would never be able to find the nursery. Instead, Kermit would have to look for him.

Kermit began to walk. He walked and walked and walked. As he walked, the snow stopped falling. The clouds parted and the moon shone down, making the snowdrifts glow. One by one, stars appeared, twinkling cheerfully.

In the sky, Kermit saw beautiful lights of pink and blue and green. *They must be the Northern Lights,* he thought as he walked toward them.

Kermit followed the lights all the way to the North Pole.

Up ahead, he spied a wisp of smoke coming from a fat red chimney that was sticking up out of the snow. He ran toward it. Then he began to dig. Soon he'd made a tunnel through the snow.

North
Pole

Kermit kept digging until he reached a big wooden door. He knocked. He heard nothing. He knocked again, more loudly this time. Still there was nothing. Finally, he knocked as loudly as he could.

Then he heard a thump, and then a shuffling sound, and then a tired little voice. "Coming, coming!" said the voice. Little footsteps trotted toward the door. With a creak and a squeak, it swung open.

Standing in the doorway was a little elf dressed in a sleeping cap and pajamas.

"Well, come in, come in," said the elf, rubbing his eyes. "Who are you? What do you want? I was asleep, you know."

"Uh, I'm sorry," said Kermit. "My name is Kermit, and I was looking for Santa Claus."

"Why, he's gone," said the elf. "It's the middle of the night before Christmas, you know. If he doesn't get an early start, he can't deliver all those presents in time. Presents that *I* help to make, I might add," the elf said proudly.

Shannon
Sandy
Paul
Kathy
Katie
Gregory
Melanie
Mark
Christopher
Emily
Ray
Joanie
Cynthia
Matthew
Nicholas
Elizabeth
Ben
Lauren
Erin
Job List
50 toy trains
93 walkie-talkie dollies
14 train sets
65 baseballs + b
05 drumsets
93 sleds
December
SUN MON TUES WED THUR FRI SAT
1 2 3 4 5 6 7
8 9 10 11 12 13 14
15 16 17 18
23 24 25
30 31
Fitz III
HARTVILLE OHIO
Little Chugger

"Oh, dear," said Kermit sadly. "Santa will never find us. There's too much snow, you see. It's covering the nursery. That's why I came–to show him the way."

"Is that why you look so gloomy?" asked the elf. "Oh, I wouldn't worry. Come over here for a moment."

Kermit followed the elf over to a big desk. Sitting on it were fat red and green books with gold lettering. The elf struggled to take one down.

A
L
K
J
D
S
R
B

"These are the directories," explained the elf. "We have addresses in here from all over the world...and Santa knows them all by heart, you know. Hmmm, let me see...."

The elf turned some pages.

"Kelvinator...Kenworthy...Kepplethwaite...Kermit! There you are! Baby Kermit. The Nursery." The elf pointed to Kermit's name in the book.

"Besides," the elf added, "Santa never gets lost. He's great at reading maps."

SOUTH AMERICA
AFRICA
Kelvinator, Fred. 319 West St.
Kenworthy, Burdett Austin. Burke
Kepplethwaite, Arthur. 866
Kermit, Baby. The
Kernal, Lou Tenant.
Keryatid, Columnea.
Kessler, Shannon. 1261
Kibender, Douglas T.,
Kildare, Richard.
Henry. 14
Amy.
Alice.
Matthew.
Nicholas.
Krohn,
Kroll,
Krosstown,
Krottinger,
Alison.

"But all the streets are covered with snow," said Kermit. "Everything looks the same. I just know he'll never find us. And Piggy and Fozzie and Gonzo and Rowlf and Scooter and Skeeter and Animal will be so disappointed."

Just then, the faint tinkle of sleigh bells drifted through the door. The elf's ears began to twitch. "It's Santa!" he shouted. "He's back!"

And sure enough–the door flew open...and in tumbled a round red figure with shiny black eyes and a button nose and a long white beard.

"You see?" sighed Kermit. "He's given up already."

"No, I haven't, young Kermit!" laughed Santa. "I came back for you."

"But how did you know where to find me?" asked Kermit.

"The same way I find all the children every year," Santa said, patting Kermit on the head. "Oh, those books and maps and things are all very well. But I find children by what is in their hearts. Every good heart sends out a light of friendship and giving that shines even in the darkest night.

"Your heart was full of love and concern for your friends. It was easy to find you."

"Now," Santa added, "if you help me, we can finish delivering all the presents before anyone wakes up. Then I'll take you home."

So Kermit helped Santa for the rest of that Christmas Eve. And when a little green frog and a man in a red suit caught the eye of a tired night watchman—well, the watchman simply rubbed his eyes and decided that he must be dreaming.

Kermit was first to wake up the next morning. He lay there for a minute, safe and snug in his bed, thinking of Santa and what he had said.

He looked around at his sleeping friends and smiled. Then he got up to welcome Christmas Day.